Other books by Mick Inkpen

One Bear at Bedtime

The Blue Balloon

Threadbear

The Great Pet Sale

Lullabyhullaballoo!

Nothing

Billy's Beetle

Penguin Small

Bear

Kipper

Kipper's Toybox

Kipper's Birthday

Kipper's Snowy Day

Kipper's Christmas Eve

Kipper's Book of Counting

Kipper's Book of Colours

Kipper's Book of Opposites

Kipper's Book of Weather

Where, oh Where, is Kipper's Bear?

Kipper's Balloon

Kipper's Monster

Kipper and Roly

Kipper's A to Z

Kipper's Beach Ball

The Little Kipper books

Wibbly Pig books

Blue Nose Island books

One year with
Kipper

Mick Inkpen

Hodder
Children's
Books

A division of Hachette Children's Books

In January
Kipper took a picture with
his new camera and made
a New Year Resolution,
'This year I will not throw
any snowballs at Tiger.'
And for a whole month
he kept his
promise. . .

Because the snow
did not fall until
February!

An icicle grew on
Kipper's house.
It lasted for three
weeks and grew
to 87 centimetres.

Kipper took a
photograph.

In **March** the wind flapped Kipper's ears.

It straightened his scarf and scruffled the daffodils on Big Hill.

Then it blew Tiger right off his feet!

Click!

This is the picture that Kipper took.

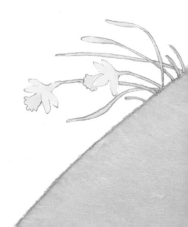

Soon the pond in the park was full of croaking and wriggling and glooping and jiggling. 'March is the froggiest month,' said Kipper.

'But April is best for catching tadpoles.'

By **May** there was blossom on the pavements thick enough to kick, and three ducklings in the park. One of them followed Tiger everywhere.

Quack!
Quack!
Click!

In June Kipper lay on his back and watched as little things with legs and wings climbed the spindly grasses and whizzed into the big, blue sky.

'There are a lot more little things with legs and wings than you would think,' thought Kipper.

The first week in
July was hot.
The second week
was hotter still.

And then Boom!

BOOOM!

BOOOM!

A thunderstorm!

August was

summer holiday time.

Kipper took a parachute
ride above the sea.

'Take my
picture!'
he called
to Tiger.

In September
the bramble bushes were full
of blackberries.

The thorns were prickly.
'Ouch! Ouch!'
But the
blackberries
were delicious.

'Mmmmmmmmm!'

In October
Kipper and Tiger made a
collection of autumn things.

'October is an orangey-
brown sort of month,'
said Tiger.

They made a face from
the pumpkin
which
glowed in
the dark.

November

came around, and twiggy branches made patterns against the misty moon.

They huffed their breath into the heavy garden air, seeing who could huff the highest.

In December the days grew dark and cold.

Kipper stayed indoors making decorations and a special Christmas present for Tiger.

'I need one more photograph,' said Kipper.

So he called Tiger and got out his camera.

'Smile!' said Kipper as he opened the front door.

But Tiger was already smiling – because it was snowing.

And because he had not forgotten about February.

Click! went Kipper's camera.

Booof!
went Tiger's snowball!

What we did this y...

February

March

May

June

July

September

October

Novembe...

April

August

December

Christmas

day came and Kipper gave Tiger his present. 'Look at me in August!' said Kipper. But Tiger was looking at December. 'This one is the best!' he said.

British Library Cataloguing in Publication Data

A catalogue record for this book is
available from the British Library.

ISBN-10: 0340 91139 5
ISBN-13: 9780 3409113 96

First published in hardback in 2006

Published by Hodder Children's Books,
a division of Hachette Children's Books,
338 Euston Road, London NW1 3BH

10 9 8 7 6 5 4 3 2 1

Colour reproduction by Dot Gradations Limited UK

Printed in China